Y0-DLJ-442

I CAN READ ABOUT
SYNONYMS & ANTONYMS

The case of strange, strange, Aunt Pickles

Written by Robyn Supraner
Illustrated by Gloria McKeown

Troll Associates

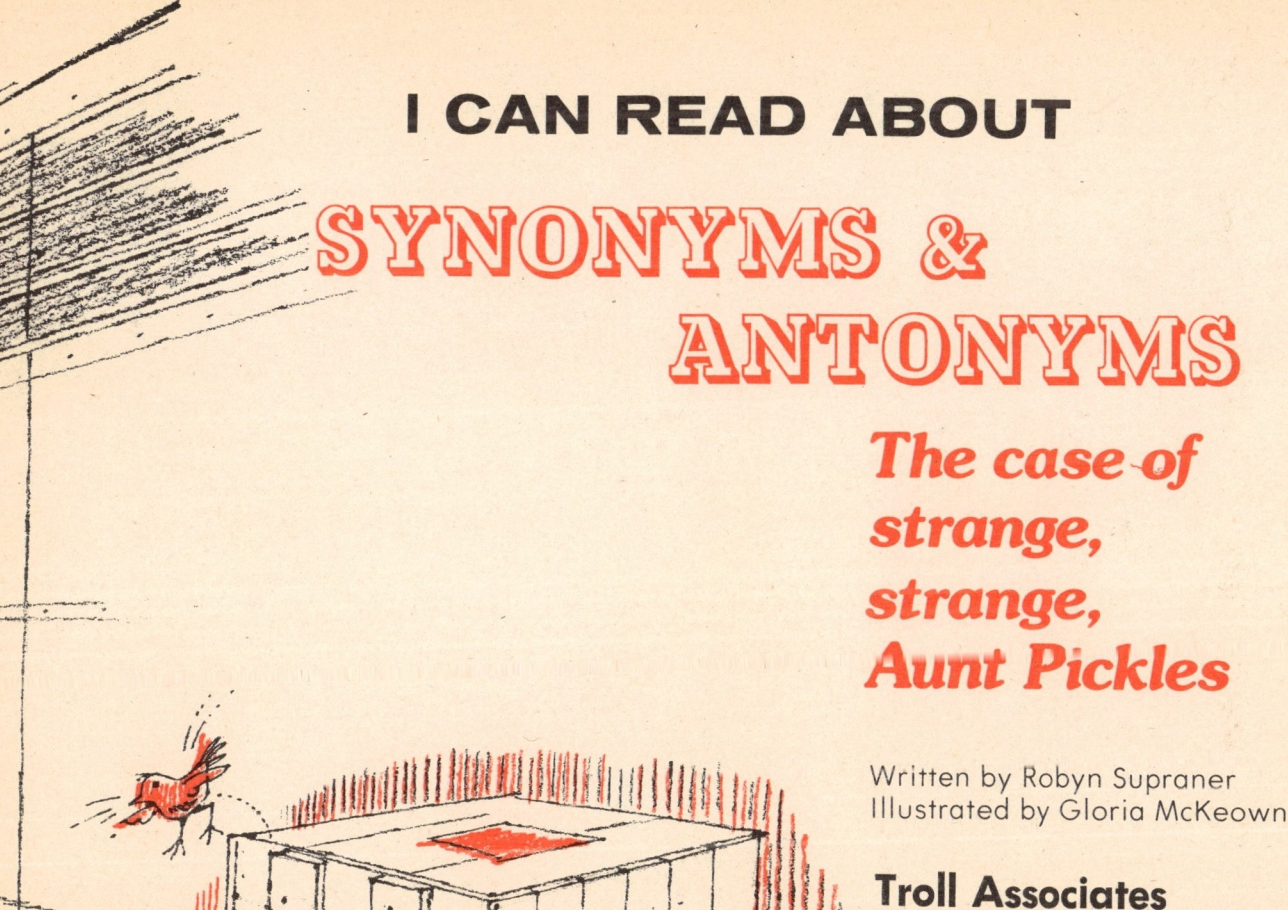

Copyright © 1977 by Troll Associates
All rights reserved. No part of this book may be used or reproduced
in any manner whatsoever without written permission from the publisher.
Printed in the United States of America. Troll Associates, Mahwah, N. J.
Library of Congress Catalog Card Number: 76-54441
ISBN 0-89375-035-2

Synthia and Synbad O'Nym were born on the same day of the same month of the same year, seven minutes apart.

From the very beginning, they were alike. They agreed about everything. And because their names began with the same three letters, they were known as the Syn O'Nym twins.

When Synthia *smiled,* Synbad *grinned.*
When Synbad *cried,* Synthia *wept.* If
one said "*ma ma,*" the other said "*mom mom.*"

If one said "*din din,*" the other said
"*yum yum,*" which meant that they
were very hungry.

When they grew older, they had the same friends.

"Sam and Sally are my *friends*," said Synthia.

"They are my *pals*," said Synbad.

"Our *chums*," said Synthia.

"Our *buddies*," said Synbad.

On sunny days they played in the yard.

"*Goodbye*," said Synthia. "I'm going *outside* to play."

"*So long*," said Synbad. "I'm going *out-of-doors*."

Then they frisked and they frolicked.
And they romped and they rollicked,
until the sky grew dark.

"It's *raining*," said Synbad.

"It's *pouring*," said Synthia.

"A *shower*," he answered.

"A *sprinkle*," said she.

"Come inside right now," called their mother. "It's *drizzling* outside."

Soon the clock said supper time.
"I'm *hungry*," said Synthia.
"I'm *starving*," said Synbad.
"I'm *famished*," she stated.
"Let's all eat!" So they all
sat down and ate a good dinner.

One day, their mother and father had a surprise for them.

"We've got a treat for you," they said. "How would you like to visit your great aunt, Pickles O'Nym?"

"*Hurrah!*" shouted Synbad.
"*Hurray!*" cried Synthia.
And though the children had not met Aunt Pickles before, they jumped up and down and clapped their hands. They said that they wanted to go.

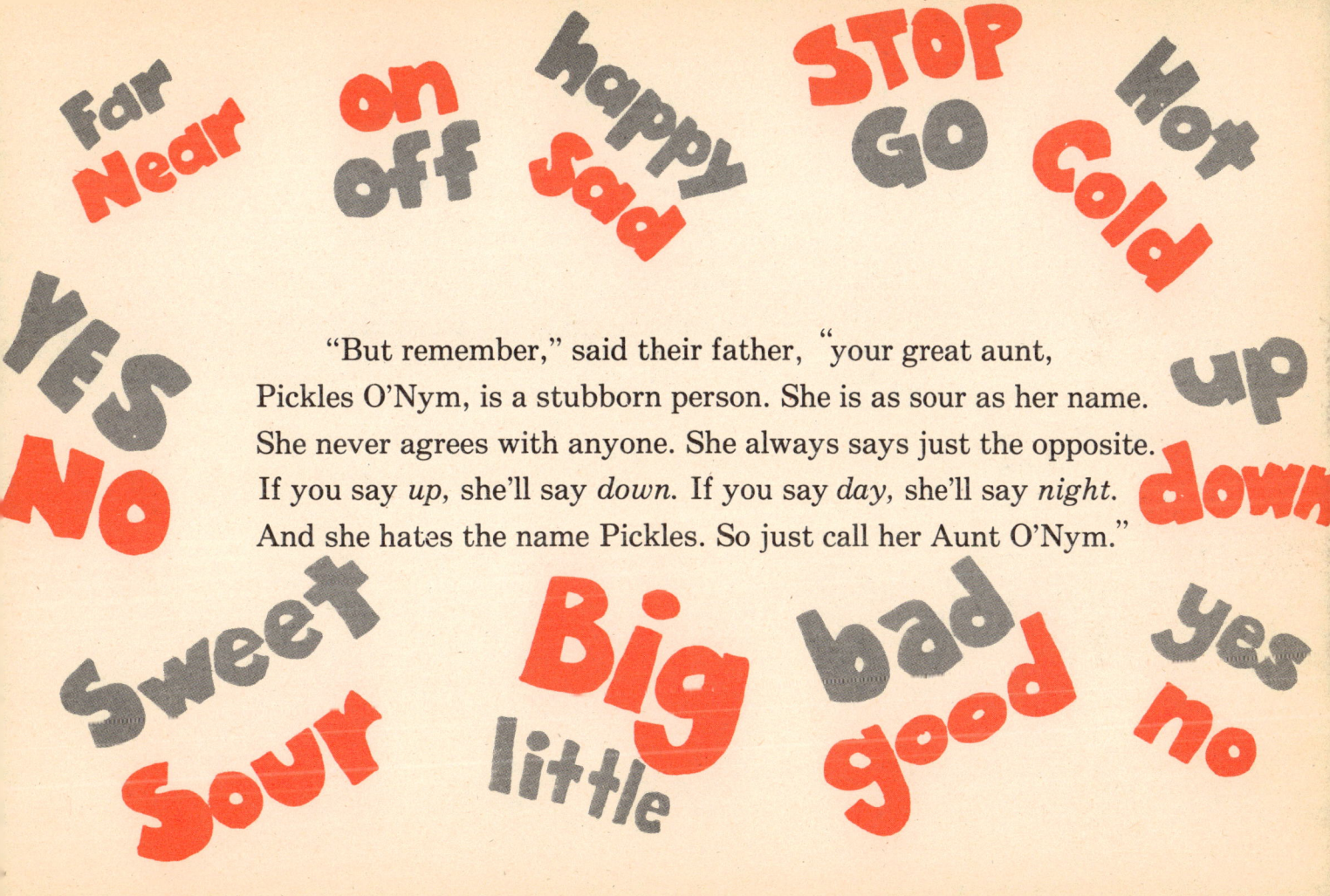

The next day the children
packed their bags and got ready
to go.
"I'm packing my *suitcase*," said Synthia.
"I'm packing my *valise*," said Synbad.

"What's taking so long,"
called mother.
"Hurry up, both of you.
Your train will be leaving soon."

When they got to the station, Mrs. O'Nym told the conductor to be sure that the children got off at Upson Downs.

The conductor smiled and told her not to worry. "Leave everything to me," he said.

Then the doors closed, the whistle blew, and the train pulled slowly out of the station.

"*Goodbye,*" shouted Synbad.
"*Farewell,*" cried Synthia.
"Have a good time," called mother and father. "Say hello to Aunt O'Nym."

"Yes, we will,"
said Synthia.
"Of course, we shall,"
said Synbad.
And the children
were on their way!

When the train pulled into Upson Downs, Aunt Pickles was there to meet them. Although the sun was shining, she wore her old galoshes and carried an umbrella.

"*Hello*," said Synthia,
as politely as she could.

"*Hi*," said Synbad,
as well-mannered as he
was able.

"Humph! . . . Hello, Goodbye,"
said Aunt O'Nym. Then
she led the way to her
car.

Putt . . . putt . . . putt . . . went her car,
up one hill and down the next. Putt . . . putt . . . putt.
Before long, they pulled up to her house.
"Well, here we are, and there you go,"
she said. "It's a good thing
I brought my umbrella
with me."

"Humph... and no wonder," grumbled Aunt O'Nym. "I've been cleaning *high* and *low*, *in* and *out*, and *over* and *under*. It's taken me most of the *day* and *night*. And to tell the truth... it's not worth it!"

The children did not know what to say. Their Aunt O'Nym was a most contrary person. Definitely disagreeable. "Well, don't just stand there," she fussed at them. "Find something to do. Go exploring. Go downstairs to the attic or go upstairs to the cellar. Just don't get *under* my feet. Or *over* my feet for that matter. Why don't you go out and play?" Then she humphed out of the room to see about fixing lunch.

The children found a basketball, and went out to play.
"What a *sourpuss*," complained Synbad.

The children found some cookies, and sat down to rest.

"What a *grump*," agreed Synthia. "We've got to figure out something."

"We've got to find a solution."

"Hey, I've got a good idea."
The children whispered together for a few minutes. Then they burst into laughter.
"It's *perfect!*" said Synthia. "A perfect plan."
"It's *excellent!*" said Synbad. "An excellent idea."
They would get even with their strange Aunt Pickles.

Humph . . . when Aunt O'Nym called them to lunch, they hurried in. "Please . . . Aunt O'Nym, we'd like our dessert *first*, if you don't mind," said Synthia.

"Humph . . . dessert is *last*," said Aunt O'Nym.

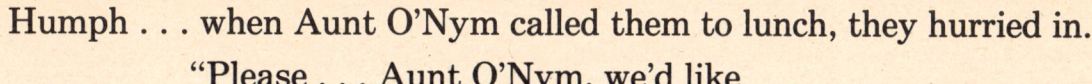

"We'd like to eat *standing up*," said Synbad.
"*Sitting down!*"
snapped Aunt O'Nym.

They both sat. Synthia tasted her sandwich.
It was delicious. "This sandwich is *bad*,"
she said to Aunt O'Nym.

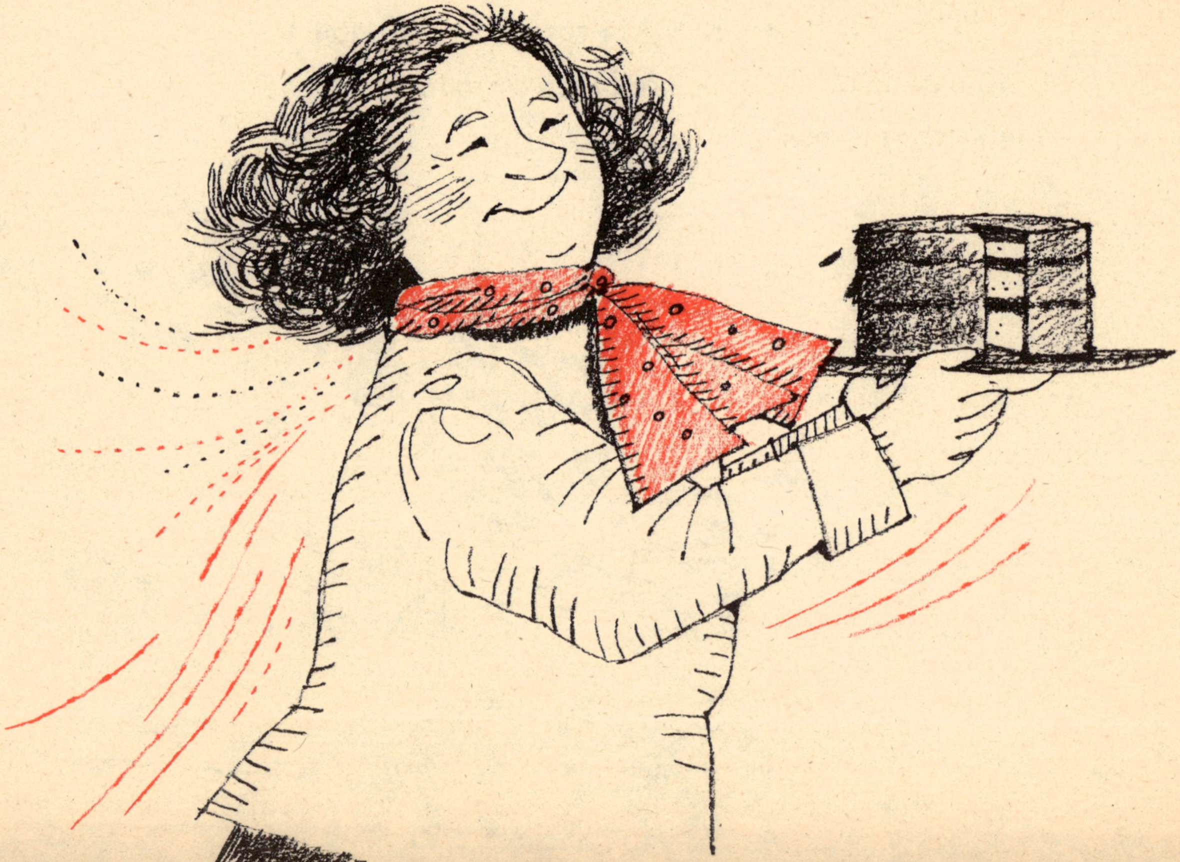

"Aha!" . . . said Aunt O'Nym. Her eyes sparkled with pleasure. "So . . . it's bad . . . is it? Well then . . . try this awful cake!"

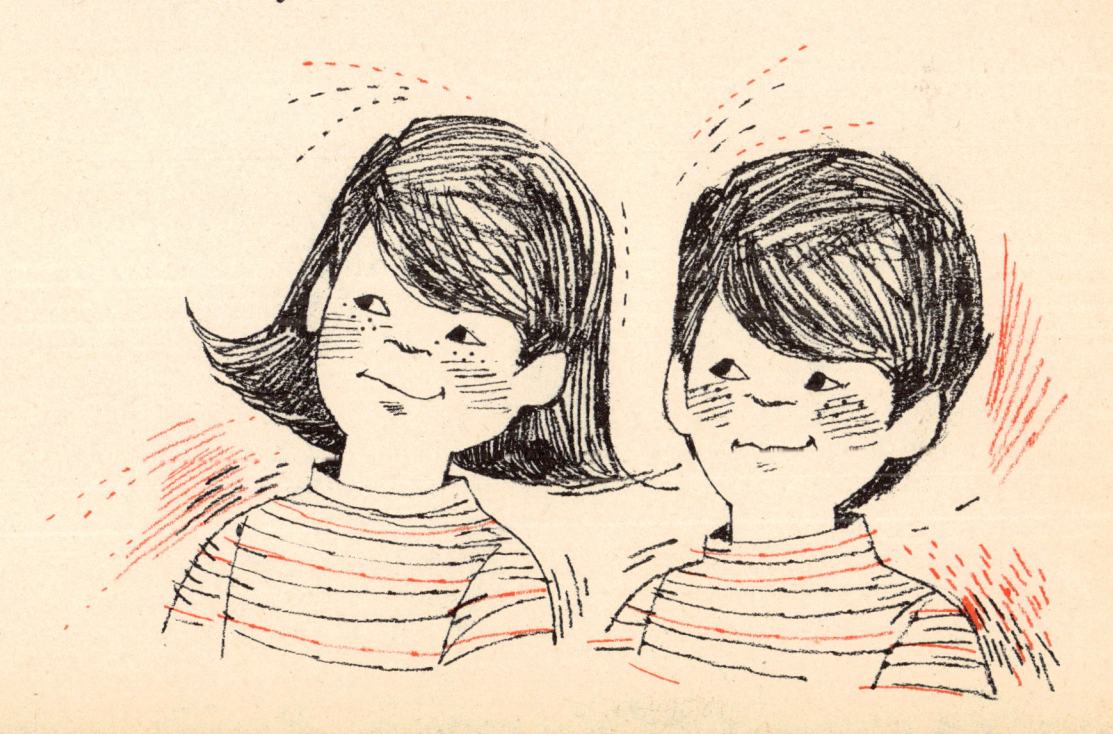

By the end of the meal, everyone was smiling and feeling friendly.

"Terrible, terrible," laughed Aunt O'Nym, but she smiled at them and passed a plate of her best apples. "I picked them myself—just for you," she said.

"You know," said Synthia, "you're really a very nice person."

"I agree," said Synbad. "You're really super!"

"Fiddlesticks," said Aunt O'Nym.

"Bosh and humbug."

Then she paused, and put her arms around them. "Humph," she said.